Captain Amelia

B.E.N.

Morph

John Silver

For information regarding permission, write to:
Disney Licensed Publishing, 114 Fifth Avenue, New York, New York 10011

ISBN 0-7172-6615-X

Printed in the U.S.A.   First printing, November 2002

Disney's TREASURE PLANET

SCHOLASTIC INC.

New York   Toronto   London   Auckland   Sydney
Mexico City   New Delhi   Hong Kong   Buenos Aires

"Fire!"

*Captain Nathaniel Flint stood on the deck
of his ship, shouting orders to his pirate crew
to attack.*

*Now yet another merchant ship was at his
mercy. Flint's men overtook the ship and
gathered up its riches. Then, just as mysteriously
as they had appeared, the pirates vanished
without a trace.*

Years passed. Flint, the most feared pirate in
the galaxy, was no more. Yet his legend grew.
Could the stories be true? Had Flint hidden the
loot of a thousand worlds in a secret place?
A place called . . . Treasure Planet.

The tale of Flint's treasure had always thrilled young Jim Hawkins. As he guided his solar surfer above the sleepy town of Benbow on the planet Montressor, Jim dreamed about finding Flint's legendary treasure.

But dreams were almost all Jim had. His father had left years ago. Jim's mother, Sarah, now ran the Benbow Inn all by herself. So things hadn't been easy for Jim or his mother.

One day, Jim went off by himself to sit on the roof of the inn. He didn't realize his life was about to change. . . .

Suddenly a spaceship crashed near the inn! Jim raced over to find a turtlelike alien named Billy Bones crawling out of the ship.

"He's after me chest! Ya gotta hide me, lad!" gasped Billy Bones. Jim helped the injured creature back to the inn.

Mrs. Hawkins and her good friend Dr. Doppler were shocked as Jim and Billy Bones stumbled through the door. "He's hurt bad. We gotta help him," Jim pleaded.

But sadly, no one could help Billy Bones. He handed Jim a strange sphere. "He'll be comin' soon . . . can't let him find this," Bones whispered. Then, with his last gasp, he gave Jim a warning. "Beware the cyborg!"

Suddenly a rumbling sound outside drew Jim to the window. Pirates were heading for the inn!

"Quick! We gotta go!" exclaimed Jim. They all escaped through an attic window as the pirates stormed the inn.

As Jim, his mother, and Doppler raced away in
the doctor's carriage, Sarah looked back in horror as
the pirates burned the inn to the ground.

When they arrived safely at Doppler's home, Jim managed to open the sphere that Bones had given him. Instantly, images of planets and stars filled the room.

"Why, this appears to be some kind of map!" said Dr. Doppler.

But it was no ordinary map. "Treasure Planet!" Jim cried when he recognized the green, two-ringed planet. The map showed the way to Flint's legendary hiding place and its treasure!

Jim was eager to go. "With that treasure we could rebuild the inn," Jim told his worried mother.

Doppler helped convince Sarah to let Jim go.

"I'll use my savings to hire a ship and a crew," the doctor offered.

Reluctantly, Mrs. Hawkins finally agreed to let Jim go with Dr. Doppler to find the mysterious Treasure Planet.

A few days later, Jim and Dr. Doppler boarded the RLS *Legacy*—the ship that would take them to Treasure Planet. There, they met the tough and quick-witted Captain Amelia. She didn't trust the crew that Dr. Doppler had hired. The Captain warned Jim and Doppler not to say anything about the map. Then she hid the map in her private quarters under lock and key.

"Young Hawkins will be working for our cook, Mr. Silver," Amelia explained to Dr. Doppler.

This decision made Jim very unhappy. And things were about to go from bad to worse. When Jim was escorted to the ship's galley, he saw the large figure of the cook standing at the stove . . . .

"A cyborg!" Jim whispered to himself when he saw that half of the cook's body was mechanical.

John Silver offered his hand. But remembering Billy Bones's warning, Jim refused to shake hands with Silver. "Jimbo! Now don't be too put off by this hunka hardware," laughed the cook, rattling his metallic arm. Then Silver introduced Morph—his playful, shape-shifting pet.

Once the ship had launched, Silver made another introduction. "Say hello to Mr. Mop and Mrs. Bucket," he told a frustrated Jim.

At first, Jim did not like working for Silver.
But over time, the cyborg taught Jim much about
life on a ship—everything from peeling potatoes
to tying knots.

Soon Jim found himself growing fond of John
Silver. And Silver grew proud of the lad as Jim
showed signs of becoming a fine spacer.

"You got the makins' of greatness in ya!" Silver
told Jim. "But ya gotta take the helm and chart yer
own course. Stick to it, no matter the squalls."

For Jim, Silver was like the father he'd never had.

Then one morning, Jim overheard Silver and the crew planning to take over the ship and find the treasure themselves. Silver and the crew were really pirates!

One pirate accused Silver of being too close to Jim. "Methinks you have a soft spot for the boy."

"I care about one thing and one thing only . . . Flint's trove!" Silver announced to his crew.

Jim was crushed. But he knew he must warn Captain Amelia and Dr. Doppler.

Suddenly a lookout on deck yelled, "Planet ho!" Treasure Planet was in sight!

The pirates dashed to the deck, but Silver returned to the galley—and saw Jim. One look told the pirate that Jim had overheard everything. So Silver blocked the exit. Quickly Jim jammed a pick into Silver's mechanical leg, surprising the old cyborg. Jim raced to Captain Amelia's cabin.

Silver wasn't far behind. "Change in plans, lads!" he bellowed to his pirates. "We move NOW!"

Captain Amelia acted swiftly when Jim barged into her quarters and told her of Silver's plans. She gave Jim the map. Then she, Jim, Morph, and Dr. Doppler escaped in one of the ship's longboats.

The pirates fired a cannon at the longboat, forcing it to crash-land on Treasure Planet. Amelia was wounded, but she knew they could not rest because the pirates would be after them.

"We need a more defensible position. Mr. Hawkins, scout ahead," she ordered Jim. And so Jim and Morph headed off into the junglelike landscape.

They hadn't gone far when a very confused robot
leaped out at Jim and hugged him. "Sorry! But after a
hundred years alone you go a little nuts!" said the robot,
who's name was B.E.N. (Bio-Electronic Navigator).

B.E.N. had belonged to Captain Flint. But the robot
couldn't help them find the treasure because Flint had
removed part of his memory chip. All B.E.N. could
remember was that the treasure was in "the centroid of
the mechanism."

B.E.N. showed Jim his home, an ancient tower on a hill. It seemed a perfect spot to hide, and Jim brought Amelia and Doppler there.

Unfortunately it wasn't long before Silver and his crew found them. The pirates captured Jim and his friends, and Silver took the map from Jim.

But Silver could not open the map, so he demanded that Jim do it for him. Jim refused.

"You want the map, you're taking me, too!" Jim insisted. Because Silver had no other option, he reluctantly agreed to bring Jim and the others along as they searched for the treasure.

With Jim in the lead, the pirates and their captives
followed the path shown on the map. Finally they
reached a cliff with strange carvings and patterns on the
ground. Jim noticed a place where the map fit like a
key. When he inserted it, a set of controls appeared.

"Have mercy!" Silver whispered. As Jim pressed the
controls, a triangular portal of light opened right in
front of them. Jim realized that the portal was a doorway
that he could make open to any point in the galaxy.

"So that's how Flint did it!" Jim declared. He
explained how Captain Flint could go anywhere, steal
treasure, and disappear back through the portal.

"But where did he stash it all? Where's the blasted treasure?" asked Silver.

Jim remembered what B.E.N. had said about the treasure being in the centroid of the mechanism. So he set the portal to lead to the planet's core.

While Doppler and Amelia were held captive, the others entered the portal. There, the most amazing sight awaited them . . . the loot of a thousand worlds!

"YEEEEE-HAAAA!" the pirates yelled.

But Jim was more interested in Captain Flint's old pirate ship. Together with B.E.N., Jim sneaked aboard. Once there, the two stared in horror.

"C-C-Captain Flint?!" gasped the robot.

Perched atop an old chair were the skeletal remains of Captain Flint! And B.E.N.'s missing memory chip was in his bony hand! Jim carefully took the chip.

"Hold still, B.E.N.," said Jim as he
plugged the chip into the robot's head.
B.E.N. shuddered momentarily,
then lit up in a big smile.

"Whoa! Hello! It's all flooding back! All my
memories! Flint pulled my memory circuit, so I could
never tell anyone about his . . . *booby trap!*"

Suddenly the entire treasure chamber began to rumble and shake.

"Run, Jimmy!" cried B.E.N. Treasure Planet was going to explode! They had to get back through the portal and off the planet—fast!

"You go back and help the captain and Doppler," Jim told B.E.N. Then Jim desperately tried to get Flint's ship to start as the treasure chamber began to collapse. The pirates fled in wild panic . . . all except Silver.

Silver had followed Jim. When Jim finally got the ship started, he was surprised to see Silver on deck.

Silver realized that Flint's treasure-filled ship was all that could be saved from the chamber now. "Ah, Jimbo!" Silver called. "Aren't you the seventh wonder of the universe!"

Jim quickly grabbed Captain Flint's sword. "Get back!" Jim yelled.

"I like ye lad, but I've come too far to let you stand between me and me treasure," said Silver.

Just then an explosion almost tipped over the ship. Silver managed to grab hold of the ship with his mechanical arm, but Jim was hurled overboard!

Flint's ship was being pulled into the fiery core of Treasure Planet. Silver planted his feet and held on to the ship with all his might. Suddenly Morph flew up to him and pointed at Jim. The boy was now hanging by one hand on the edge of a deep crevice!

Silver had to make a choice: he could save either the treasure or Jim.

"Arghhh! Blast me for a fool!" exclaimed Silver. He truly cared about Jim and couldn't desert him now. Silver let go of the ship and caught Jim just in time.

Together, Jim, Silver, and Morph made it back through the portal and onto the *Legacy*. Amelia, Doppler, and B.E.N. had outwitted the panicky pirates and regained control of the ship.

"Hurry, people! We've got exactly two minutes and thirty-four seconds until the planet's destruction!" yelled B.E.N.

"We'll never get away in time!" shouted Doppler.

But Jim had an idea. If he could get back to the portal's controls, he could get it to open to another place in the galaxy. Sailing through the portal would bring them all to safety.

With Silver's help, Jim quickly created a makeshift solar surfer.

Jim then surfed off the ship and
headed through the self-destructing planet,
straight for the control panel.

The others steered the ship directly into the giant
triangle. With only seconds left, Jim reached the
controls and changed the portal's destination!

As Treasure Planet exploded, the *Legacy* sailed through the portal to safety. Jim followed closely behind.

Everyone else cheered as Jim landed safely on deck.

"Didn't I say the lad had greatness in him?!" Silver shouted proudly.

"Unorthodox, but ludicrously effective!" Amelia agreed. She even said that she would be happy to recommend Jim to the Interstellar Academy.

"Just wait until your mother hears about this!" exclaimed Dr. Doppler.

Jim turned to look at Silver, but the cyborg was gone.

Jim soon found him with Morph in the hangar bay, untying a longboat. Jim knew Silver had to leave to avoid going to prison, so Jim opened the hatch of the bay.

"What say ya ship out with us?" Silver asked.

Jim shook his head. Silver had taught him to believe in himself, and now Jim had his own dreams to pursue.

The old cyborg understood. "You're gonna rattle the stars, you are!" Then Silver handed Jim some treasure he'd managed to save. "For your dear mother, to rebuild that inn of hers," Silver explained.

Then, leaving Morph with Jim, the cyborg sailed out into the etherium.

After rebuilding the Benbow Inn, Jim and his mother threw a party. Jim proudly wore the uniform of the Interstellar Academy. With a bright future ahead of him, Jim looked up gratefully at the stars. There he saw a glimmer of the pirate who had helped him find the greatest treasure of all—the treasure within himself.